Bakers on Board

The Cupcake Club

Sheryl Berk and Carrie Berk

sourcebooks
jabberwocky

Copyright © 2016 by Sheryl Berk and Carrie Berk
Cover and internal design © 2016 by Sourcebooks, Inc.
Series design by Rose Audette
Cover illustration © Kristi Valiant

Published by Sourcebooks Jabberwocky, an imprint of Sourcebooks, Inc.
P.O. Box 4410, Naperville, Illinois 60567-4410
(630) 961-3900
Fax: (630) 961-2168
www.sourcebooks.com

Library of Congress Cataloging-in-Publication Data

Names: Berk, Sheryl, author. | Berk, Carrie, author.
Title: Bakers on board / Sheryl Berk and Carrie Berk.
Description: Naperville, IL : Sourcebooks Jabberwocky, [2016] | Series: The
    cupcake club ; [book 9] | Summary: In exchange for tickets on a Caribbean
    cruise ship, Jenna and her friends in the cupcake club must bake 12,000
    cupcakes for a pirate-themed event.
Identifiers: LCCN 2015032234 | (13 : alk. paper)
Subjects: | CYAC: Cupcakes--Fiction. | Baking--Fiction. |
    Friendship--Fiction. | Clubs--Fiction. | Cruise ships--Fiction.
Classification: LCC PZ7.B45236 Bak 2016 | DDC [Fic]--dc23 LC record
available at http://lccn.loc.gov/2015032234

Source of Production: Versa Press, East Peoria, Illinois, USA
Date of Production: February 2016
Run Number: 5005974

Printed and bound in the United States of America.
VP 10 9 8 7 6 5 4 3 2 1

Thank you to Aunt Peggy
for always cheering for us!

Surprise, Surprise

Jenna Medina's stepfather, Leo, came through the door of their house singing a happy tune: "Sailing, sailing, over the ocean waves…" He kicked up his heels and did a little jig around the living room. For the finale, he jumped up on the couch and bowed deeply.

Jenna giggled. By now, she was used to Leo's silliness. A year ago, when her mom sprang it on her that they were getting married, his jokes and teasing had driven her crazy. But that was before Jenna knew him—and decided to give him a chance.

"I grow on you, kind of like mold," he'd teased her on the big wedding day in Las Vegas. "Please let me show you what a great papa I can be."

Leo *had* shown her, in more ways than one. He was always there for her when she needed to make a delivery for her cupcake club. He was there when she was sweating over her science final and needed someone to test her on the elements of the periodic table. He'd even convinced her *mami* to let her adopt Dulce, her Havanese puppy. Her own father had left her mom to raise five kids by herself, but Leo had assured Jenna that he would never leave. He had an enormous heart, and Jenna had grown to love him, as well as her new stepsister, Maggie, who stayed with them every other weekend.

Leo had found them all a bigger home so Jenna didn't have to share a bedroom with her two older sisters, Marisol and Gabby. Even if her room was small, she actually had some peace and quiet and privacy away from her maniac little brothers, Ricky and Manny. It was all hers—from the patchwork quilt her *mami* had sewn from Jenna's old baby blankets to the Oreo cookie pillow her BFF Kylie had given her, because like an Oreo, "she was a tough cookie outside and a softie inside." Having her own space was a dream come true. Now, she could cover her walls with pictures of her favorite Spanish telenovela stars and not worry that Gabby would draw mustaches on all of them!

Yet there was no denying her family was more loco than most. Especially when Leo called for a family meeting.

"What is it, *mi amor*?" Her mother, Betty, came racing

out of the kitchen, still carrying a raw chicken in her hands. "*Qué es la emergencia?*"

"Mami, are we having *arroz con pollo* for dinner?" Ricky asked, tugging on her apron.

"No! I want pizza!" Manny protested. Jenna's five-year-old siblings never could seem to agree on anything.

Gabby skipped downstairs. Her hair was set in hot rollers. "Can we hurry it up? I'm meeting Marc at the mall."

Jenna rolled her eyes. All her sister thought about—and talked about—were boys!

Leo took a head count. "So, Maggie is at her mom's tonight, and I will have to call her with the good news. But where's Marisol?" No doubt Jenna's oldest sister had her nose in a book upstairs.

"I'll go get her," Jenna volunteered. She raced up the stairs and barged right into Marisol's bedroom, even though her door was shut.

"Hey!" Marisol yelled. "Do you ever knock?"

"Nope," Jenna said, shrugging. "Leo wants you downstairs—*ahora*!"

"I'm just finishing up," Marisol said, focusing on something on her laptop screen.

"*Qué pasa?*" Jenna asked, peering over Marisol's

3

shoulder. She assumed her sister was working on yet another term paper that would earn her yet another A+.

"None of your business," Marisol replied, slamming the computer shut. "I'll be right down."

Once everyone was gathered, Leo cleared his throat. "*Mi querida familia*, the Medina-Winters clan," he began. Jenna tried to stifle a laugh but it was hard. Leo loved to speak in Spanish—although he wasn't very good at it. "As you all know, my boss, the *fabuloso* fashion designer Ralph Warren, has been looking for a unique venue to premiere his new resort collection."

Jenna did know. Leo took great pride in his vice president of marketing position and talked about it all the time. His passion for fashion was one of the things that had drawn him and Betty together. He had come into the tailor shop where she worked one day by chance and spotted her beautiful sewing. According to him, it was love at first stitch.

"Well, I've found it. And I am going to take all of you along with me on this trip," he continued. "If you guess where it is."

"Paris? Are we going to Paris?" Gabby asked excitedly.

"Good guess," Leo teased her, "but no cigar."

"London? Milan? New York?" Marisol picked up where Gabby left off, naming the rest of the fashion capitals of the world.

"No, no, and no." Leo shook his head. "You're not even warm—which is a hint." He winked at Jenna.

"Warm? So the location of your runway show is someplace warm?" she asked. "Like tropical warm?"

"*Sí! Estás cerca*," he teased. "You're close."

"A beach!" Ricky piped up. "I wanna build a giant sand castle."

"Think more surf, less sand," Leo hinted.

"Hawaii? Are we going to Hawaii?" Betty jumped in. "I've always wanted to see it."

"No, not Hawaii." Leo grinned mischievously. "I'll give you another hint: I'm sure this collection is going to make a big splash."

"Water!" Jenna exclaimed. "Is it the rain forest?"

"You're missing the boat." Leo winked. "Think harder."

While the rest of her family was completely baffled, Jenna suddenly remembered the sailor song Leo came in singing. "Sailing… Missing the boat… Wait, are we going on a cruise ship?" she guessed.

"Ding-ding-ding! Give that girl a prize!" Leo cheered. He handed her a brochure that read "Victory Cruises" and showed a photo of a giant white ship with seventeen decks. "Yes, we are all going on a seven-night cruise to the Bahamas over midwinter break from school!"

Anchors Aweigh

"You are so lucky," Kylie told Jenna when she broke the cruise news at lunch in the Blakely Elementary cafeteria the next day. She had brought the brochure Leo gave her to school to show her friends.

"Ralph Warren bought out the entire cruise for a corporate retreat so they can present the new spring-summer line to the company," Jenna said proudly. "Leo is organizing the entire thing."

"It looks amazing," Kylie said. "I can't wait to tell the cupcake club!"

"I know you're president of Peace, Love, and Cupcakes and all," Jenna said gently. "But it's my cruise. Let me do the telling, *por favor*?"

"Oh sure," Kylie replied. "You can tell the girls."

Sadie sat down next to them. "Tell me what? What did I miss?"

"The fact that Jenna is going on a cruise to the Bahamas with her family in two weeks!" Kylie was so excited she wouldn't let Jenna get a word in. "Can you imagine? It's like a giant hotel floating on the water."

"Sweet!" Sadie replied. "That'll be so much fun. I saw this cruise ship commercial, and the ship had ginormous rock climbing walls."

Jenna shook her head. "No, no rock climbing for these feet." She pointed to her sneakers. "You're the jock, Sadie, not me."

Lexi dropped her tray down at the table next to Kylie. "Ugh, do you think the cafeteria lady could even *consider* the art of food presentation?" She groaned. "Honestly! She just threw my mac and cheese on top of my hot dog. It's gross!" Since Lexi was the cupcake club's official cake decorator, she bristled anytime anyone presented a plate that was less than pretty.

"You won't believe Jenna's amazing news," Kylie began. But this time, Jenna put her hand over her friend's mouth.

"Yes, it's *my* news," she reminded Kylie. "So let me tell Lexi."

"She's going on a cruise ship!" Sadie blurted out. "And it has like a dozen restaurants and a kids' club and a giant waterslide and three pools… Oh, and a magic show at night!"

Jenna threw her hands in the air. "I give up!"

"Sorry, Jenna," Sadie apologized. "It just slipped out. But you can tell Delaney and Herbie at the PLC meeting after school." Since Delaney attended another school and their advisor taught robotics all day, the club met once a week at 3:30 p.m. in the Blakely teachers' lounge.

"Oh, I kinda emailed them both just now," Lexi said, holding up her phone. "Sorry. I couldn't wait."

Jenna shook her head. "I am surrounded by *bocas grandes*, big mouths! Remind me never to ask any of you to keep a secret."

"And *you're* such a great secret keeper?" Lexi teased her. "How about the time I told you I had a crush on Jeremy Saperstone and you blabbed it all over the place."

Jenna blushed. "Okay, fine. I might have told a few people."

"Me!" Kylie said.

"And me," Sadie added.

"And the entire fifth grade," Lexi pointed out. "I'm just sayin'."

Delaney and Herbie were equally excited by Jenna's announcement—even if it came through Lexi's email.

"Can you take me with you, please!" Delaney pleaded as she burst into the Blakely teachers' lounge. "Maybe smuggle me on board in one of your suitcases?"

"A cruise ship that size has a very complicated computerized system," Herbie added thoughtfully. "Maybe you should bring me along too—in case of any glitches."

Jenna shook her head. "Sorry, guys. Leo only has eight tickets—enough for him, my mom, my sisters and brothers, and our stepsister, Maggie."

"No problem," Kylie reminded the club. "We're going to be very busy over break. Remember? We said we're going to work on a new PLC website to show off our cupcake creations and drum up more business."

Delaney scowled. "Well, Jenna's break sounds like a lot more fun."

Kylie opened her official cupcake club binder to an order labeled "Mount Vernon Library" and showed it to her friends. "Any ideas for this one?"

Lexi read the client's request carefully: "Twelve dozen cupcakes commemorating our forefather's influence on our great country."

Delaney's eyes lit up. "Hey, maybe we could make a life-size replica of the Lincoln Memorial out of cupcakes."

"Oh no," Lexi exclaimed. "Not happening. I went to DC with my family a few years ago, and that Lincoln is almost a hundred feet tall!"

"That's taller than Sadie," Jenna teased.

"Nice idea, wrong president," Kylie interrupted. "Mount Vernon was George Washington's home, and this is the library's annual fund-raiser cocktail party."

Lexi heaved a sigh of relief. "In that case, I think we should bake something elegant—but with presidential flair."

"What do you think of when you think of George Washington?" Herbie asked them. "I'll admit American history was never my best subject."

"Mine neither," Sadie said. "But I do know he got in trouble as a kid for chopping down his father's cherry tree. When his dad asked him if he did it, he said, 'I cannot tell a lie!'"

Delaney made a face. "Ooh, busted! I bet he was grounded for a week."

"How did you ground a kid in the seventeen hundreds?" Kylie wondered out loud. "They didn't have TV or Xbox or iPhones to take away. It must have been really tough to come up with a punishment."

"This cupcake design is really tough to come up with

too," Lexi said, chewing on her pencil eraser. "We could do red, white, and blue—but that seems so boring."

"What about red, white, and blueberry?" Jenna suggested. "Cherry vanilla cupcakes, our famous white chocolate cupcakes, and blueberry cobbler cupcakes?"

"Okay, I'm liking this direction," Kylie replied. "Keep going."

Lexi held up her sketchpad. "I could do a silhouette of Washington out of fondant," she said. She'd used a charcoal pencil to show how the silver gum paste would look when molded to resemble the first president.

Jenna took a quarter out of her pocket and compared it to Lexi's drawing. "That's pretty good—but don't forget the bow on his ponytail. And make it strong and commanding—not floppy."

Lexi added a ribbon to the bottom of George's do. "Happy now?"

Jenna smiled. "*Sí! Muy feliz.*"

Kylie put a check next to the order in her book. "Then all that's left is for us to get baking."

Taste Test Time

After two years of running a successful cupcake business, Peace, Love, and Cupcakes had gotten recipe testing down to a science. Jenna was in charge of the ingredients and tasted every cupcake to make sure it was *delicioso*. Sadie was the expert egg cracker and in charge of whipping the batter to a perfect, smooth consistency—without overbeating it.

Lexi was the artist—the one who made sure every cupcake was frosted neatly and delicately with just the right ratio of icing to cake. She created intricate decorations sculpted out of fondant or modeling chocolate, and Delaney was her right-hand woman, standing over each cupcake, ready to give them the finishing touch: a dusting of sprinkles, mini chips, chopped nuts, coconut, candies, or even—in this case—shimmery edible glitter.

"What do you think?" Delaney asked, holding up a

cupcake for Kylie to inspect. Everyone's opinion mattered in the cupcake club, but it was Kylie's job to give it the presidential seal of approval.

"I love it—it's so shimmery, like a medal of honor," she said.

She handed the cupcake to Jenna to sample. "Cherry vanilla up first."

Jenna used a fork to sample the inside of the cupcake. They had blended chopped maraschino cherries into the batter and topped the frosting with a long-stemmed cherry.

"Nice," she said, licking the fork. "Nice texture—very moist. But I would up the amount of cherry syrup just a bit—I'm losing the cherry flavor to the vanilla."

She took a bite of the frosting by itself. "I'm liking the texture." Finally, she tried both cake and frosting together.

"Well?" Kylie asked anxiously. "What's the verdict?"

Jenna smacked her lips together. "*Sabroso.*"

Delaney scratched her head. "Translation, please?"

"Tasty!" Jenna exclaimed.

The white chocolate cupcake was one of their most popular recipes, so Sadie and Delaney knew the ingredients and directions by heart.

"Six ounces white chocolate, melted!" Sadie called across the kitchen.

Delaney placed a bowl in the microwave and watched it carefully, checking every thirty seconds to make sure the chocolate didn't burn. She whipped it with a whisk until it was smooth and glossy.

"Aye, aye, captain," she said, pouring the hot chocolate into the mixing bowl with the batter. Then she turned to Jenna. "See? I would be totally amazing at sea. I already know sailor lingo." She saluted and announced, "Shiver me timbers!"

Kylie cracked up. "That's pirate lingo, Laney," she said. "I don't think Captain Jack Sparrow is going to be cruising with Jenna."

But Jenna was too busy trying to figure out the blueberry cobbler cupcake recipe. "The question is, how much blueberry pie filling do we put in the batter?" she said. "Too much, and you get a mushy cupcake. But too little, and you lose the whole blueberry flavor."

She looked at the muffin tins filled with cupcake liners. "Batter first, then *un poco* blueberry filling on top," she decided.

"What's a *poco*?" Delaney asked, studying her measuring spoons. "Is that like a teaspoon?"

"*Un poco*. It means 'a little,'" Jenna said. "In this case, a little more than a teaspoon but a little less than a tablespoon."

"I'm confuzzled," Delaney said. "I thought we should never guess ingredient amounts."

Herbie weighed in. "Yes, baking is a science. Precise measurement is key."

"You're both right, but I gotta go with my gut here," Jenna insisted. "Have I ever steered us wrong?"

The girls looked to Kylie for her decision. "Jenna is our official cupcake taster. What she says goes."

When the cupcakes came out of the oven twenty minutes later, Jenna gently removed one from the tin and placed it on a plate to cool. She peeled the wrapper back and squeezed the warm cake gently with her fingertips. "Spongy—not mushy. So far, so good."

Then she took a bite.

"Well?" Lexi asked. "Don't leave us in suspense."

Jenna didn't say a word. She took another bite. Then another, and another.

When she had devoured the entire cupcake, she wiped the blueberry stain off her mouth with a napkin. "It's not good," she said slowly.

Kylie's face fell. A bad recipe meant back to the drawing board. "Really? Not good at all?"

"No," Jenna said, sighing. Then she smiled brightly. "*Es perfecto!*"

She handed each of the girls a cupcake. "Try it. I think it's one of the best recipes we've ever made."

Delaney, Lexi, Sadie, Herbie, and Kylie each dug in. Like Jenna, they couldn't speak—they were too busy gobbling up every last crumb.

"Yummo," Sadie finally said. "Is that a Spanish word?"

Jenna chuckled. "No, but it sums it up perfectly."

"The fund-raiser is a week from Saturday," Kylie said, checking her binder. "Which means we bake Thursday, decorate Friday, and deliver Saturday afternoon."

"And I set sail the next day," Jenna pointed out.

"Go ahead, rub it in," Delaney said, groaning.

Jenna picked up a piping bag and squirted a dollop of pink frosting in the palm of her hand. Then she rubbed it across Delaney's nose and cheeks. "You said to rub it in," she teased.

Delaney shrugged, wiped the frosting with her finger, and took a lick. "*Un poco* messy, but still yummo," she said, laughing.

Picture This

Kylie and the girls were packing the red, white, and blue-berry cupcakes in the back of her dad's car when her phone suddenly rang.

"Is this Peace, Love, and Cupcakes?" a harried woman asked on the other end.

"Yes, it is," Kylie replied. "But we're about to make a delivery. Can we call you back?"

"It's the delivery that I'm calling about," the woman continued. "The cupcakes for the Mount Vernon Library fund-raiser. This is Ms. Cushman, the head librarian."

"Oh, yes!" Kylie replied. "We'll have them there soon. Five o'clock sharp, just like we promised."

"There's a little problem," Ms. Cushman said, hesitating. "It seems we underestimated how many guests would be coming tomorrow. We need a few more than I originally ordered."

"Not to worry," Kylie said. "We always bake some extras just in case. Instead of twelve dozen, you have thirteen dozen."

"That's nice of you," Ms. Cushman said. "But I'm afraid we need more than that for our guest list."

Kylie held up her hand, motioning for Jenna, Sadie, Lexi, and Delaney to stop loading the car. "Exactly how many more cupcakes are we talking about?" she asked.

"Oh, just another twelve dozen."

Kylie's mouth hung open. "Are you serious? You need us to double the order? Now? We can't!"

Sadie grabbed the phone out of her hand. "What she means is we can't—unless you pay us a rush fee. A dollar more per cupcake."

"Fine," Ms. Cushman said. "I'll wait for you to get here. But please hurry. My favorite show, *History Chronicles*, is on TV tonight and I never miss an episode." She hung up.

"Sadie, are you crazy?" Kylie gasped. "We can't bake and decorate twelve dozen more cupcakes. It took us three hours yesterday to get this batch done—and it's already four o'clock."

"I don't even think we have enough ingredients left over," Jenna piped up. "We're low on berries, big-time."

"It's a lot of money," Sadie pleaded. "And I've had my eye on a new bike for the summer."

"We've been in a cupcake crunch before," Delaney insisted. "We can do it if we work together."

"Let me think," Kylie said, pacing back and forth. If there was one thing she was good at, it was dealing with a cupcake crisis. "We'll leave these cupcakes in my dad's car. It's cold out here, so they'll be fine as long as we don't move them. Jenna will ask her sister Marisol to drive her to the market while the rest of us get to work on the fondant toppers."

Lexi shook her head. "I have to roll out fondant for another hundred and forty-four Georges?" she complained. "My poor aching wrists."

"We'll all help," Kylie assured her. "If we're gonna do this, it has to work like an assembly line. Sadie cracks; Delaney mixes; you and I roll."

Jenna gave her the thumbs-up. "I texted Marisol and she's not thrilled, but she's on her way."

When Marisol pulled up in her car she had a scowl on her face. "You owe me," she told her younger sister as she jumped in and buckled up.

"It's not like you have anything better to do," Jenna teased her.

"For your information, I was working on something very important."

Jenna yawned. "What? A physics experiment? Memorizing *War and Peace*?"

"No, nothing to do with studying," Marisol replied.

Jenna looked puzzled. "Did I interrupt you alphabetizing your book collection?" she joked. "*Lo siento!* I'm so sorry!"

"Forget it," Marisol said in a huff. "You wouldn't understand anyway." She pulled up in front of the market and clicked the door lock open. "Go on. I'll wait for you here."

Jenna actually felt a little bad for teasing her sister. Something was clearly bothering her.

"Okay, I'll be quick," she said, jumping out. "Thanks for the ride."

Marisol shrugged. "Whatever."

When they returned to Kylie's house, the kitchen was in full swing. "Bring those berries over here," Sadie said, motioning to the mixing bowl. "We're ready for them." It took them two hours to bake all three flavors and another hour to frost and decorate. It was nearly seven o'clock before they were ready to hit the road for Mount Vernon.

"Marisol said she'll help us drive them over," Jenna told her friends. "Though she's not very happy about it—or anything actually."

"Great. My dad's backseat is packed to capacity," Kylie said. "Let's box 'em up and get them loaded."

There was only enough room for two passengers in each car: Kylie and her dad, and Marisol and Jenna.

"I win Father of the Year for this," Mr. Carson said, getting his keys. "And you're lucky it's not a school night. It'll take us at least an hour to get there—if there's no traffic, but there will be on a Friday night."

"I'll make it up to you," Kylie promised. "You can sleep late tomorrow morning, and I'll make you pancakes."

"With some of those leftover blueberries?" he asked, turning on the ignition. "Now you're talkin'!"

The trip took them longer than expected. When they finally arrived at the library, it was eight thirty. Kylie knocked on the door, but it was locked and no one answered. She peered through the window and saw that everything was dark and quiet inside.

"I thought Ms. Cushman said she would wait for us," Jenna said, carrying a stack of boxes out of the car.

"She also said she never misses an episode of *History Chronicles*," Kylie recalled. "Which started a half hour ago."

"Now what?" Marisol grumped. "It's freezing out here, and we've got three hundred cupcakes and no one to accept them."

"I suggest we drive down the road and find a neighbor willing to hold them for Ms. Cushman till tomorrow morning," Mr. Carson suggested. "Or it won't be just the cupcakes that freeze."

They all piled back in and drove to a small house just down the street from the library. Kylie rang the doorbell and crossed her fingers.

A gray-haired man opened the door a crack and peeked outside. "May I help you?" he asked.

"I hope so!" Kylie exclaimed. "We have to deliver these cupcakes to the library but it took longer than we thought to mix the batter and Jenna had to buy berries and then we hit traffic and Ms. Cushman left to go watch her TV show."

The man scratched his bearded chin. "I'm not sure what you're talking about," he said. "But if you're selling cupcakes, I'll take one."

"No." Kylie tried to explain better. "They're for the library's annual fund-raiser tomorrow night. We're not selling any, but if you can hold on to them for Ms. Cushman to pick up tomorrow, we'll gladly give you one."

The man opened the door the rest of the way. "I know Ms. Cushman very well, and I'll let her know I have them," he said. "You can bring them into the kitchen and leave them there for her."

He motioned to a room down the hall. "It's right through there, past the photos on the wall."

As they all piled past him carrying box after box, his eyes grew wide. "I thought it was a dozen or so cupcakes...not enough for General Washington's army!"

"Sorry," Kylie apologized. "Ms. Cushman asked us to double the amount at the last minute, so I'm afraid there's a whole carload more."

"You might want to stack those in the living room," he suggested. "It's a pretty small kitchen."

As Marisol walked by, she couldn't help noticing all the amazing framed pictures. "Wow, did you take these?" she asked.

"I did," the man said. "I used to be a professional photographer. In fact, the library has a few of my shots on display."

She put the boxes down and walked back to get a better look. "They're amazing. Like something out of *National Geographic* magazine."

"You have a good eye. I used to shoot for *National Geographic*." He pointed to the signature in the corner of the print. "That's me. Harold Hammond."

Marisol continued to study the pictures. There were several of a desert at sunset, one of lions lounging in the Serengeti, and yet another of the view from the top of the Eiffel Tower.

"I worked in Paris for quite a while shooting fashion models for magazines," he said. "In my younger days."

"It must have been incredible to travel the world and see all these sights," Marisol said. "I wish I could."

"It was quite an adventure," Mr. Hammond reflected. "But now I've retired and hung up my cameras." He seemed sad. "I'm older now. That's all behind me."

"You must miss it," Marisol said. "I don't know how you could ever give this up."

"Are you a photographer?" he asked, changing the subject.

"Oh, just an amateur one," she said, showing him a few photos on her phone. "Besides, I'm applying to college this year."

"Those are pretty good." He nodded. "You have real talent. If you're interested, I know some people at the Los Angeles Film School, where I went. I could put in a good word for you. They have an amazing photography department." He handed her his business card from his wallet.

"That's so kind," she said. "But my mother has her heart set on me going to medical school one day."

"And what is *your* heart set on?" Mr. Hammond asked.

"Photography does seem very exciting," Marisol said, thinking out loud. "I just don't know if I can…"

"You see this?" He showed her a picture of a dolphin flying high above the waves off the coast of Oahu. "My editor told me to get this shot. I said, 'I don't know if I can.' And he told me, 'You can…but are you willing to do what it takes?'"

He patted Marisol on the back. "I put the same question to you."

Jenna found Mr. Hammond and Marisol talking in the hallway. "Here you go," she said, handing him a white chocolate cupcake. "Thanks again for letting us crash our cupcakes overnight."

"My pleasure," he said, taking a lick of the frosting. "Happy to help out. Nice meeting you all and reminiscing."

☆ ☮ ☆

All the way home, Marisol seemed absorbed in thought. She stared ahead at the road and said nothing.

"You and that photo guy seemed to hit it off," Jenna commented. "What were you talking about all that time?"

"Stuff," Marisol said simply.

"What sort of stuff?" Jenna asked.

"Just stuff. It's none of your beeswax."

Jenna shrugged. "Well, you can think about your *stuff* all you want. The only thing I'm thinking about is setting sail on our cruise Sunday morning."

"Maybe I'll bring my camera," her sister said suddenly. "Do you think we'll see any dolphins?"

Jenna just couldn't figure Marisol out these days! "Dolphins? Since when do you care about dolphins?"

"There's a lot I care about," her sister insisted. "You and your friends have your cupcakes, but what do I have?"

"Amazing grades, for one thing," Jenna said.

"I mean something that makes me *really* happy. Something I can get excited about."

"I'd get excited if I had straight As," Jenna said. She couldn't understand why Marisol seemed so worked up.

They pulled up in front of their home, and Marisol shut

off the car's lights. "Please don't say anything to Mami or Leo," she pleaded. "I'm just being silly."

Jenna promised, but she had a hunch that Marisol wasn't being silly at all. She was being very serious.

An Itchy Situation

Bright and early Saturday morning, Jenna came downstairs to eat breakfast. There was no time for sleeping late: she had last-minute packing to do for the cruise the next day.

"I'm not sure how much sunscreen to bring." She poured herself a bowl of cereal and sat down next to Marisol at the kitchen table. "I'm planning on lounging by the pool a lot."

"Uh-huh," Marisol said, distracted. She was on her laptop again.

"Did you hear a word I said?" Jenna asked, annoyed. She hated when her sister tuned her out.

"What?" Marisol said, finally looking up.

"What are you so busy with anyway?" Jenna asked, trying to catch a glimpse of the screen.

This time, Marisol didn't slam it shut. "Can you keep a secret? A big one?" she asked her youngest sister.

Jenna gulped. She remembered what Lexi had said about her not being a great secret keeper. "I can try," she said.

"No, you have to pinkie swear you will tell no one," Marisol insisted. She held up her pinkie.

"Okay, okay, I pinkie swear," Jenna said, linking their little fingers together. "What's the huge secret?"

Marisol sighed. "Well, you know how Mami always talks about me being a doctor one day," she began.

"It's 'cause you're supersmart," Jenna replied. "You'd make a great doctor."

"True," Marisol joked. "I am brilliant. But I've been doing a lot of thinking. I couldn't sleep last night after I talked to that photographer, Mr. Hammond." She turned her computer screen around to face Jenna. On it was an application for a photography scholarship to the Los Angeles Film School—the school Mr. Hammond had told her about.

"Los Angeles? You want to go to college in California?" Jenna exclaimed.

"Shhh!" Marisol hushed her. "Do you want to wake up Mami and Leo?"

"Mami is going to freak," Jenna insisted. "What happened to going to Stamford or Wesleyan, not somewhere so far from Connecticut?"

"I think I'm going to apply for a scholarship," Marisol said quietly. "Mr. Hammond says my photos are really good." She clicked on a picture on her desktop that showed shadows dancing across the grass in their backyard.

"Wow," Jenna said. "That *is* good."

"So do I apply for the scholarship…or not?"

Jenna had no idea what to advise her sister—it was usually Marisol's job to advise *her*. But she was honored that Marisol had asked her opinion, so she wanted to give it a lot of thought. On one hand, she was all for following your dreams wherever they took you. But on the other hand, she knew the news of Marisol moving across the country— and not becoming the first doctor in the Medina family— would upset her mother terribly.

"*No sé*," Jenna replied. "I don't know what to tell you. It's a really tough decision."

Marisol nodded. "I know. I've been so torn that I haven't even packed yet for the cruise."

"That's okay," Jenna said. "I'm sure Gabby hasn't put a single bikini in her bag yet. I better go wake her up."

Marisol went back to reading up on the Los Angeles Film School's photography curriculum. "Thanks," she told Jenna.

"For what?" Jenna asked. "I didn't do anything."

"You listened," Marisol replied. "And you didn't judge."

"Follow *sus sueños*," Jenna told her sister finally. "Follow your dreams. Like you said last night in the car, you need to do something that makes you feel excited. If film school is what you want, I think you should do it. Mami will understand. She wants you to be happy."

When Jenna knocked on her other sister's bedroom door, all she heard was snoring coming from inside. "Gab, time to rise and shine," she called. "Only twenty-four hours till cruise time."

There was no response—not even Gabby's usual "Get out! Leave me alone!"

Jenna poked her head in and found her sister buried under the covers. "Okay, lazybones, time to get up." She pulled the covers back and saw Gabby's face, which was covered in tiny pink dots.

"*Dios mío!*" Jenna exclaimed. "What is that?"

Gabby opened one eye and yawned. "What's what?" Her hand touched her face and unconsciously began scratching.

Jenna grabbed a mirror off her dresser and handed it to her. "Your face. It's polka-dotted!"

Gabby bolted up in bed and stared in the mirror. "No! It can't be!" The more she looked at the dots, the more they began to itch.

Her mother, Leo, and Marisol came running into the room to see what all the commotion was about. "*Dios mío!*" Betty shouted.

"You can say that again," Marisol said, her mouth hanging open. "Your face looks awful!"

By now, Gabby was hysterical. "I know it looks awful! I look like one of Leo's ties!" she sobbed.

Leo tried to calm everyone down. "My ties aren't that bad, and neither is chicken pox. I had it; your mother had it."

"I thought I had a shot for it," Gabby wailed.

"*Sí,*" her mother replied. "Which is why you won't have a bad case and will heal very quickly."

"It's not fair," Gabby said, scratching furiously at the red dots on her arms and legs.

Manny and Ricky came into their room in their pajamas. "Mami, I feel hot," Ricky said, holding his head and sniffling.

"And I feel itchy," Manny added, scratching at his stomach.

"Oh no, not you too!" Betty said, examining the twins.

"Is it the chicken pops?" Manny asked. "Priscilla in our class got it last week."

"I don't like chicken pops. I like lollipops," Ricky whined.

"I'm so sorry, *mi amor*," Betty told Leo. "It's very bad timing."

Gabby sniffled. "What do you mean 'bad timing'?"

Leo sat down on the side of her bed. "You can't go on the cruise with chicken pox, and neither can Manny and Ricky." Leo looked at his wife. "What will we do?"

"You go with Jenna, Marisol, and Maggie. I will stay here and take care of everyone," Betty insisted.

"I feel terrible," Leo said, taking Betty's hand. "And I have four extra tickets now."

Jenna suddenly got a brilliant idea. "Four? That's perfect! That's exactly how many I need," she said.

Leo looked—as Delaney would say—confuzzled. "Perfect for what?"

"For taking Sadie, Lexi, Delaney, and Kylie on the cruise. Please, Leo? Pretty please? If we get everyone's parents to agree?"

Leo scratched his head. "On one condition: Peace, Love, and Cupcakes bakes cupcakes for our big pirate-themed party onboard."

Jenna threw her arms around him and gave him a huge bear hug. "You are the best! *El mejor!*"

Before he could change his mind, Jenna raced to her room to call Kylie.

"I have great news," she said excitedly. "My sister and brothers have the chicken pox, and PLC is setting sail tomorrow!"

Sea You Later

Kylie, Delaney, Sadie, and Lexi had to do some quick convincing, but twenty-four hours later, they were joining Jenna on the cruise.

"My mom said I have to write my social studies report while we're on the ship," Sadie announced.

"What's it on?" Lexi asked as they waited in line at the ship terminal in New York City.

"That's the problem—I have no idea what to write about," Sadie said, sighing.

"How about how *long* it takes to board a cruise ship," Jenna replied impatiently. Besides going through security and checking passports, they each had to wait till their cabin assignments were ready. Leo ran around with a clipboard, making sure everything his marketing team had ordered was being loaded aboard the ship.

"What about the balloons? The giant Ralph Warren

logo banner? The confetti cannon?" he asked his assistant, Mitchell.

"Yes, sir, all accounted for," Mitchell answered. "And just in time. He's here! He's here!"

Ralph Warren, the famous fashion designer, pulled up to the ship's terminal in a long, black stretch limo. He was dressed impeccably in a navy suit and a red, white, and blue tie with tiny anchors on it.

"Leo!" he said, shaking Jenna's dad's hand warmly. "I can't tell you how much I'm looking forward to this collection launch—especially the runway show at sea."

"You are? I mean, you are!" Leo replied nervously. "We all are. It's going to be amazing."

"We hope," Mitchell muttered under his breath.

"I'll see you onboard then," Mr. Warren replied. "Anchors aweigh!"

Leo mopped his brow with a handkerchief and began checking and double-checking his clipboard for the third or fourth time.

"Dad looks a little frazzled," Maggie said.

"It didn't help that half our family is home sick with chicken pox," Jenna said. "He felt terrible leaving Mami. And she was so disappointed."

Marisol overheard their conversation and gulped. She, too, was worried about disappointing Mami. What if she told her mother she didn't want to be a doctor and Mami burst into tears? Or worse, what if she decided to be a photography major—and Mami grounded her for life? What then?

"Next!" a cruise agent bellowed, waving his hand in Marisol's face. "Unless you want the ship to set sail without you, young lady?"

"I'm sorry," she said, handing him her passport and ticket. "I was just daydreaming."

Jenna tapped her on the shoulder. "You should take lots of pictures on the cruise," she whispered. "You know, in case you need some to send with your scholarship application to film school."

"I haven't decided if I'm applying," Marisol said, looking around to make sure Leo wasn't in earshot. "I told you to keep it a secret, so don't blab."

"Blab what?" Delaney poked her head in between them. "What's all the whispering about? Did I miss something?"

"Nada," Jenna said. "Marisol was just wondering if they have a chocoholic buffet at midnight tonight."

Delaney's eyes grew wide. "Chocoholic buffet?" she gasped. "Now those are two words I love to hear."

The girls all got their cabin assignments and waited for Leo to board the gangway with them.

"Daddy"—Maggie waved at him—"are you coming?"

Leo was shouting loudly into his phone. "Isn't there anything you can do? Hire a private jet or something? Mr. Warren just boarded the ship. What am I supposed to tell him?"

"Uh-oh," Maggie said, watching her father's face turn bright red. "Something's wrong."

"Qué pasa, Leo?" Jenna asked him gently.

He waved her off and continued yelling into the phone. "What am I supposed to do? Who is going to photograph the collection? You've left me in a terrible bind!"

When he had finished with his conversation, he turned to his family and friends. "Major *problema*. Patrick De Olivier, the famous photographer I hired to shoot the new collection, missed his flight this morning from Paris. Now he'll never make it here before we sail."

"I'm sure you can find someone else to take pictures," Kylie said, trying to cheer him up. "I mean, there must be a gazillion photographers who could do it."

"On this short notice? When we're sailing in less than three hours? I doubt it." Mitchell echoed his boss's concern. "This is a disaster."

"Beyond disaster," Leo said, sighing. "I could lose my job for this."

Marisol suddenly remembered Mr. Hammond telling her how he got his start shooting the runways in Paris. "I know someone who might be able to help you," she told Leo. "He gave me his card." She pulled it out of her purse.

"Okay, I'm desperate. I'll try anything," Leo said, handing the card to Mitchell to call. "Let's hope 'Harold Hammond, Professional Photographer' has no plans for the next week."

☆ ☮ ☆

There was only an hour left before the ship set sail, and Harold was still nowhere in sight.

"All ashore who are going ashore," a crewman's voice rang over the loudspeaker.

"What could be taking him so long?" Leo asked anxiously.

"Maybe he's stuck in traffic," Mitchell suggested. "Or maybe he needed a little nap."

Just then, they saw a gray-haired man in Bermuda shorts and a Hawaiian shirt inching his way up the gangway. He was pulling a suitcase on wheels and carrying a large bag filled with cameras and lenses over his shoulder.

"It's him! It's him!" Leo said, relieved. He raced over to give the photographer a hand.

"I made it," Harold said, out of breath. "That was a close one!" He extended his hand to Leo to shake. "Thank you so much for the opportunity. It's been ages since I had an assignment."

Leo tried not to let on how nervous he was. "Yes, well, thanks for coming. I hope you're up to it."

"Up to it? This isn't the first Ralph Warren runway show I've worked," Harold boasted. "I shot his resort line at Paris Fashion Week in the nineteen eighties."

"Oh, how lovely," Mitchell muttered under his breath. "He hasn't taken fashion photos in thirty years."

"I'm sure you'll do a great job," Leo said, patting Harold on the back.

"Where's my assistant?" Harold asked, looking around.

"Assistant? You didn't mention anything about needing an assistant," Mitchell replied.

"A photographer always needs an assistant."

Mitchell was practically hyperventilating. "The ship is sailing in five minutes. Are we supposed to make an assistant magically appear out of thin air?"

"Marisol will do just fine," Harold replied.

Leo looked stunned. "Marisol? My Marisol? My step-daughter? You must be mistaken."

"No, I'm not," Harold insisted. "She showed me some of her work Friday night when the girls were at my house. I'd love to hire her for the cruise to assist me."

Leo shrugged. "I guess… I mean, if she wants to."

"I have a hunch she might," Harold said, winking. "In the meantime, I do believe you mentioned a private cabin with a balcony and a chocoholics buffet."

He handed Mitchell his suitcase. "Lead the way!"

7

High Seas Hijinks

The ship was way larger than Jenna had ever imagined. "I got lost trying to find my way back from the elevator to my cabin," she told her friends. "Those hallways are a mile long!"

"Did you see all the restaurants? And the pool? And the waterslide?" Delaney gushed. "It's like a floating city at sea."

"There's a basketball court, a shuffleboard deck, even a video arcade," Sadie said, studying the map the cruise director had given her. "I don't know what to do first!"

"I do," Kylie said. "I'm scouting out the galley—that's 'kitchen' in ship-speak. Leo said the pirate party will be a huge event with fireworks and laser lights projected on a huge screen above the pool. And we have just a few days to prepare for it."

"Do we have any details—anything I can start thinking about for cupcake decorations?" Lexi asked.

Kylie nodded. "It's a salute to all the great pirates on the Seven Seas, from Bluebeard and Captain Kidd to Hook and Jack Sparrow. Our cupcakes have to be equally spectacular—and dastardly."

Jenna rubbed her temples. "I'm sensing some crazy Kylie cupcake stunt," she said. "We're not going to shoot them out of a cannon, are we?"

"That's not a bad idea…" Kylie contemplated. "But I think they'd be hard for people to catch, don't you?"

"What if we shish-kebabbed a bunch of cupcakes on a giant pirate sword?" Delaney suggested. "Then we could have a bloody battle on the high seas!"

"Ouch! That sounds dangerous!" Lexi protested. "And it would make holes in all my cupcake art."

"Bloody and gory is cool," Kylie said. She had seen every Pirates of the Caribbean movie twice. "But I think Lexi is right. Swords might scare the guests."

"Fine, it was only a suggestion," Delaney said. "I just think it would be fun to stage a pirate sword fight." She pretended to wave a sword in the air and laugh like an evil pirate. "Yo-ho-ho!"

"Yo-ho-*no*!" Jenna said, shaking her head. "Think presentation. What would make a big splash at the party?"

Kylie thought hard—but was interrupted by Maggie.

"How long till it's warm enough for us to swim?" she asked Kylie. "I brought this big raft to blow up but it's freezing on deck."

"We'll be two days at sea before we hit Florida sunshine," Sadie reminded her. "But it's fine—there's so much to do on the ship. I'm hitting the rock climbing wall tomorrow morning."

Maggie flopped down in a chair next to her. "I just want to float on my raft in the pool and soak up some rays."

Suddenly, Kylie had a brilliant idea. "What if we built a huge raft with a sail and put hundreds of mini cupcakes on it, right smack in the middle of the pool?"

"You mean sail our cupcakes into the pirate party?" Jenna asked her.

"Exactly! Maybe it could start out in the dark with some fog and scary music—like the *Flying Dutchman* in Pirates of the Caribbean? It's crewed by the undead!"

"That's creepy," Sadie said. "But cool."

"I could do a skull and crossbones in fondant on each of them," Lexi added.

"Good!" Kylie exclaimed. "What about flavors?"

"Jolly Roger raspberry," Jenna said. "And pirate pistachio!"

"And we could all dress up like pirates with eye patches and fake mustaches," Delaney chimed in.

"I think we have a game plan," Kylie said. "A floating cupcake ghost ship and pirate costumes for all."

Leo made sure the girls of PLC had full access to the ship's "junior" galley—a second kitchen that was free while the cooking staff worked in the main one preparing meals. While the other guests enjoyed all the activities the ship had to offer—lectures, concerts, auctions, and unlimited food and fun—Kylie insisted the girls get down to business.

"What happened to sun and fun?" Delaney complained as they rummaged through the enormous pantry for ingredients.

"It's still too cold on deck," Kylie reminded her. "You'd be sunning in a ski jacket."

"It's not too cold to rock climb," Sadie grumped. "By the time we finish here, the line will be a mile long!"

"Cupcakes come first," Kylie reminded them. "We need to nail down the recipes, build the raft, and then bake and decorate. We'll have plenty of time for other stuff tomorrow or the day after."

"Fine," Delaney said. "But after the pirate party I'm off duty. All cupcakes and no play make Delaney a grumpy girl!"

They experimented with several variations on a raspberry cupcake: raspberry on the inside; raspberry on the outside; fresh raspberries chopped and sprinkled throughout the batter.

Jenna took a bite and examined the cupcake closely. "It looks like our cupcake has the chicken pox," she commented. "It's all polka-dotted."

"What if we pureed the raspberries first?" Kylie suggested. "Less chunky, more smooth?"

Jenna found a bottle of raspberry extract on a galley shelf. "And this will ensure we get that punch of raspberry flavor."

"Okay," Kylie said, checking off her list. "On to the pistachio ones."

Sadie placed a huge ten-pound bag of pistachio nuts on the counter. "The recipe calls for the nuts to be shelled." She took out a single nut, cracked it open, and popped it in her mouth. "This is gonna take a while."

"What about frosting?" Jenna asked. "Brown sugar buttercream? Cream cheese frosting?"

"No," Kylie insisted. "It needs to be something dark and sinister…like dark chocolate ganache."

"Easy," Jenna replied. "And Lexi's skull and crossbones can sit right on top."

Leo came in the galley to check on them. "How are the cupcakes coming along?" he asked. "I'm sure they'll be the hit of the pirate party."

"Slowly and surely," Kylie said. "We've got the recipes worked out. Now we just have to bake them. How many exactly should we make?"

Leo checked his guest roster. "I'd say we need twelve to cover everyone," he said.

"Twelve dozen cupcakes?" Delaney asked, surprised. "That's nothing! We can do that in our sleep."

"Not twelve dozen," Leo corrected her. "Twelve *thousand* cupcakes. There are over three thousand people on board."

Kylie gasped. "That's one thousand dozen! I'm not sure we've ever done an order that big before."

"Well, you've never been on a cruise ship this large before," Leo pointed out.

"*No problema*," Jenna assured him. "We promised and PLC always keeps its word. Right, guys?"

Kylie's head was still spinning, but Jenna had a point. They had promised Leo an amazing cupcake display in exchange for the trip. "Right. I guess. Sure."

"Okay, then I'll leave you to it, ladies. I have to go find Harold and Marisol and make sure they're all set to shoot the runway show tomorrow."

Kylie checked the oven. It was a huge industrial one, capable of baking twelve dozen cupcakes at a time. She clicked the calculator on her phone and did some quick math. "Okay, so we can bake twelve dozen every twenty-two minutes, which means we can bake a thousand dozen in about 1,833 minutes…"

Lexi rolled her eyes. "Um, that's like thirty hours. And that doesn't even include the time we need to frost and make all the fondant toppers."

"OMG, we're going to be working for two days straight!" Sadie groaned.

"And we have to build the raft and sail too," Lexi reminded them. "That's several more hours."

Kylie sighed. It was an awfully big assignment. "Well, no use sitting around complaining," she said. She cleared her throat and did her best Johnny Depp British pirate accent. "Like Captain Jack Sparrow always says, 'The problem is not the problem. The problem is your attitude about the problem.'"

"Translation?" Jenna asked.

"Let's make this fun!" Kylie exclaimed. "Isn't that what PLC is all about?"

Delaney took a handful of flour and sprinkled it over Kylie's head. "How fun is that?" she asked, slightly annoyed. "Certainly not as fun as the shuffleboard tournament on Deck 8."

"You guys, you're missing the point," Kylie insisted. "We're here together, and we've got a ginormous kitchen to play in." She gestured around the galley. "Would you just look around you?"

Sadie walked over to a huge mixer and flipped it on. It whizzed to life. "This is pretty awesome," she said.

Delaney opened the enormous refrigerator room door. "Whoa!" she said, noting entire shelves filled with eggs, milk, and butter. "There's like an entire grocery store in here."

"And will you just check out all these bottles of food coloring?" Lexi asked, admiring the pastry chef's collection. "Who knew blue came in so many shades?"

Delaney seized a wooden spoon and thrust it at Kylie.

"Avast, ye landlubber! I challenge ye to a duel to the death on the high seas," she said.

Kylie picked up a spatula to defend herself. "Arrr, no one challenges Cap'n Kylie Sparrow. Else you want to walk the plank, me bucko?"

"Shiver me timbers, me thinks we need a high-seas shanty fit to duel to," Delaney continued. She improvised a funny pirate song:

"Yo-ho-ho and a bottle of vanilla,

we have more than 12,000 cupcakes to filla!

But fear we not, 'cause mighty we are.

All hands in now, and let me hear you say 'Arrr!'"

"Arrr!" the girls sang out, roaring with laughter.

"Delaney, you are one crazy pirate captain," Kylie said, dropping her spatula on the counter. "I surrender!"

Delaney bowed. "Me hat's off to you, Cap'n Kylie. You said we could make this fun, and you were right."

"We can make anything fun if we do it together," Kylie said, holding up an empty muffin tin. "Time's a-wasting, maties."

8

Picture This

The next morning, as Harold unpacked his camera bag, Marisol carefully laid each lens, flash, and tripod out on the floor of the Neptune lounge to inventory them.

"What's this?" she asked, holding up something that looked like an umbrella.

"It's a reflector," Harold replied. "Very important in lighting a subject."

"There's so much I don't know about photography," Marisol said. "It's overwhelming."

"It comes with time," Harold assured her. "When I started out, I wasn't much older than you. The best thing you can do is just take pictures. You learn from doing."

He handed her an old Nikon camera. "I traveled with this all over the world. It was one of my first cameras. Good old Lucy never let me down."

"Lucy? You name your cameras?" Marisol asked, giggling.

"Sure do! That one there is Ethel, and these two are Betty and Veronica."

"Okay, Lucy," Marisol said, putting the camera strap around her neck.

Harold had an idea. "Tell you what. Why don't you hang on to her for a while for me and take her out for a spin?"

"Really?" Marisol said, admiring the camera's intricate lens. "You sure you wouldn't mind?"

"Just keep a close eye on her," Harold warned. "Lucy's a delicate old girl."

Marisol wandered around the ship, snapping shots of various guests enjoying themselves. There was a woman admiring an ice-sculpting display; a group of little girls playing ring-around-the-rosy in the kids' center; and an older gentleman asleep on a deck chair. She noticed that the air on the top decks wasn't as chilly as it had been when they left New York. In fact, it was almost warm. They must have been getting closer to Florida and the Bahamas. She gazed out at the rolling waves and breathed in the salty air.

"Hey, Maggie!" she called, spotting her stepsister walking around with an ice cream cone in her hand. "Where'd you get that from?"

Maggie pointed to an ice-cream parlor way on the other side of the deck. "DIY cones," she said. "All you can eat, open twenty-four seven!"

She offered Marisol hers. "I'll give you my cone if I can hold your camera for a sec."

Marisol hesitated. "It's kind of on loan…so be very careful with it," she instructed Maggie. Maggie threw the strap over her neck and peered through the lens. "Whoa, this thing really zooms!"

"Pool's open!" a little boy yelled, racing past them.

"No way!" Maggie squealed. "Finally!" She took off after him, forgetting she was still holding Lucy.

"Wait! Maggie!" Marisol shouted after her and dropped the cone. "Don't get the camera wet!"

But it was too late. Maggie was standing at the edge of the pool watching as the boy did a cannonball off the side. In a split second, he soaked her from head to toe.

"Hey! Why don't you watch where you're splashing!" she yelled at him. She looked down at the camera dangling from her neck. "Oh no. I got it wet!"

Marisol caught up to her and snatched Lucy back. She tried drying the camera off in a towel, but no matter how many times she tried to switch it on, it wouldn't oblige.

"Maggie, you ruined Lucy!" she moaned. "What will l I tell Harold?"

"Who's Lucy? Who's Harold?" Maggie asked. "I'm really sorry. I didn't mean to, honest!"

Marisol sighed. "Lucy is the camera, and Harold is the photographer who trusted me with her. I guess it's just as much my fault as it is yours. I shouldn't have let it out of my sight."

"Well, maybe Harold will know how to fix it," Maggie suggested.

"Oh no. I couldn't possibly tell him I broke his precious camera. I'll just have to keep my mouth shut and hope I can fix it before he finds out." She tucked Lucy into her tote bag. "He's got a lot on his mind with shooting the collection anyway."

When Marisol caught up with her photo mentor, he was busy in the main ballroom, taking test shots and checking the lighting with a meter. There was a long runway for the models to walk down, and red velvet curtains with glistening gold Ralph Warren *RW* logos framed the stage.

"It's not ideal," Harold said, noting how the light

streamed in through the room's small portholes, streaking the walls. "But we can make do."

"I've seen a runway show before," Marisol said, reflecting on the time Leo took her and Gabby to New York Fashion Week. "It was really dark with lots of flashing lights."

"Exactly," Harold said. "Which means I supplement the flash and change my focus mode—since the models will be moving fast and I don't want my subjects to blur."

Marisol nodded and pulled out her pen and paper to take notes. Harold was so smart!

"The show is supposed to start at 8:00 p.m., right after the banquet dinner," she said, checking the schedule. "Sounds fancy."

"Then you better go get yourself gussied up," he pointed out. "I'm good here."

"Okay—if you're sure you don't mind," she said. She did want to straighten her hair, do her makeup, and figure out what shoes to wear with the evening gown Mami had made her.

"Go on, have some fun. It's your vacation," he told her. "Take some great pictures with my Lucy. Can't wait to see 'em."

Marisol gulped. She felt awful that she had ruined Harold's camera! "Um, yeah, great…" She hesitated. "I'll do that."

Great, Marisol thought to herself as she went back to her cabin. *I'm not only lying to Mami, but I'm lying to Mr. Hammond as well!* She bumped smack into Leo, who was walking down the hall with his nose in his clipboard.

"Oh, hi, *mija*," he said. "I hear the pools are open."

"Yeah, they certainly are." Marisol couldn't help groaning. If it weren't for the pool, she wouldn't be in this predicament.

"I thought you'd be psyched for a swim," Leo replied, puzzled. "I can't get Maggie out of the water."

"Too much splashing going on for me," Marisol said, dashing off before Leo asked any more questions. "Don't wanna ruin my hair."

Leo shrugged. His stepdaughter's strange behavior was the least of his worries. The fashion show was set to start in just a few hours, and most of his models were unaccounted for.

"Leo to Mitchell… Come in, Mitchell," he said in his walkie-talkie. "Have we tracked down all ten of the ladies for the fashion show?"

"Negative." Mitchell's voice cracked and hissed over the receiver. "I'm short one of them. I've looked everywhere—the spa, the pool deck, the game room, the lunch buffet. If you were a model, where would you be?"

"Keep looking," Leo instructed him. "I need her in hair and makeup in less than an hour. Or Mr. Warren is going to have both our heads on a platter at the banquet tonight."

9

Tall Tales

Somehow, Jenna, Kylie, Sadie, Lexi, and Delaney managed to get themselves cleaned up and dressed for the banquet. They had been working practically nonstop for two days on the pirate cupcakes, and none of them were in any mood for a fancy five-course dinner—much less a fashion show and after-party. But Leo insisted they all be at his table at 5:00 p.m. sharp.

"I'm so tired." Lexi yawned, taking her seat. "I dozed off in the shower and dreamed I was rolling out fondant."

"Can I just take a quick nap?" Delaney asked, resting her head on the table. "Just a few minutes."

Kylie elbowed her. "If I'm staying awake, so are you."

Just then, they all heard snoring from across the table. It was Jenna, who'd fallen fast asleep in her bread plate.

"Jenna! Wake up!" Kylie gave her a kick under the table.

She jumped to attention. "What? Huh? I'm coming, Mami!"

Kylie chuckled. "I'm not your *mami*. And you should probably wipe the drool off your chin. It doesn't go with your dress."

Embarrassed, Jenna dabbed her face with a napkin. "*Estoy tan cansado!*" she said. "Translation: All I wanna do is crawl into my bed and sleep for a week."

"If you did that, you'd miss the whole cruise," Marisol pointed out. "Not to mention the fashion show I'm helping Harold photograph."

"Yay, you." Jenna tried to sound enthusiastic as she stifled a yawn.

"How many more cupcakes do we have left to decorate?" Sadie asked. "I lost count at 7,200."

"I figure if we do another five hundred tonight, we can finish off the rest tomorrow."

"We'll be in Florida tomorrow," Lexi pointed out. "It's gonna be hot and sunny, and we're going to be stuck in a kitchen dipping cupcakes in ganache?"

"There's a day excursion to Disney World," Delaney reminded them. "Roller coasters and spinning teacups and Mickey Mouse…oh my!"

"Mickey will have to wait," Kylie insisted. "We have to get the raft built and stacked with cupcakes. Plus the rest have to be plattered for the waitstaff to hand out."

Jenna's head once again hit the table and she started snoring. "*Despertarse!*" Marisol said loudly in her ear. "Wakey, wakey."

"No!" Jenna moaned in her sleep. "No more bakey, bakey!"

Marisol gave her hair a sharp tug and Jenna jumped to attention. "Ouch! No hair pulling!"

Marisol giggled. "Works every time."

Just then, Leo took his seat at the head of the table. "Is everybody looking forward to a delicious gourmet meal?" he asked. He was dressed in a black tuxedo.

Kylie tried her best to smile. "Mmmmm, can't wait."

Before they could even dig into the first course—a delicious goat cheese and cranberry salad—Mitchell came running into the dining room to find Leo. He looked frantic.

"We're down one model for the show," he told Leo. "She's in her cabin with horrible seasickness."

"What?" Leo gasped and pushed his plate away. "She can't be."

"Trust me," Mitchell replied. "Unless you want her to walk down the runway clutching a barf bag, it's not happening."

"This is awful," Leo said in a panic. "The clothes have already been fitted. Where are we going to find a five-foot-ten model to wear Mr. Warren's design?"

Jenna suddenly perked up. "You need someone five-foot-ten?" she asked. "What about Sadie?"

Sadie dropped her fork. "Me? I'm not a model. I'm a basketball player."

"A super-*tall* basketball player," Kylie chimed in. "You could totally do this."

Leo looked worried. "It's kind of you to offer, but Sadie's never walked a runway before."

"How hard could it be?" Jenna said. "You just put one foot in front of the other, right?"

Mitchell and Leo stared at each other, then at Sadie. "It might work," Leo finally said. "It will have to."

Mitchell grabbed Sadie by the arm. "Come with me," he instructed her. "No time to waste."

"But…wait…" Sadie stammered as he ushered her out of the dining room. "Can we talk about it? I'm not sure!"

"Pass the butter," Jenna said, smiling. "I'm staying awake for this."

After dinner, the guests poured into the ship's grand ball-room. There were three levels of seats, and every single one was taken. Leo had saved the girls seats in the front row along the runway.

"This is so exciting for Sadie," Delaney said. "I'm jealous."

Marisol hovered behind Harold as he got into position at the end of the runway. "Let's just hope it's smooth sailing," he told her. "I've never shot a fashion show at sea before, and my hands aren't as steady as they used to be."

There was no time to hesitate. Leo appeared on the stage to introduce the start of the program.

"Esteemed guests and fellow company employees," he began. "It is my great privilege to introduce our host for this evening as well as the entire cruise, Mr. Ralph Warren."

The designer took the stage in a red plaid dinner jacket. "Thank you," he said. "I'm very excited to debut my latest collection. I call it 'Over the Ocean Blue.' I hope you enjoy it."

The lights dimmed and strange whistling noises filled the room.

"What is that?" Kylie whispered.

"I think it's a dolphin singing," Lexi replied. "Either that or nails on a chalkboard."

"Ya think he played that *on porpoise?*" Jenna joked with her friends. "Get it? Dolphin? Porpoise?"

The first model walked out on the stage wearing a cat-suit covered in silvery-blue scales.

"Something's fishy!" Jenna continued to crack herself up. This fashion-show business was a lot more fun than she had thought it would be!

Harold reached his hand behind him to Marisol. "The light is reflecting off the scales," he said. "I think I need Lucy for this one."

Marisol's heart jumped. "Lucy? You need Lucy?"

"Yes," he insisted. "Don't you have her? I told you to not to let her out of your sight."

Marisol dug in her tote. "I know, and I have her…" she said, gently handing the old camera back to Harold. "But there's something I have to tell you."

Harold threw the camera strap around his neck. "Later," he said. "I don't want to miss this shot."

Marisol held her breath as he clicked the camera on. Amazingly, it came to life.

"Good ol' Lucy!" she cheered.

When all the other models had glided down the runway in their blue nautical-themed fashions, it was time for Sadie to make her debut.

"Mitchell said she was the last model," Delaney said excitedly. "This is it!" She perched herself on the edge of her seat.

The soundtrack shifted to the sounds of waves crashing on a beach, and a spotlight hit the back of the runway. There was a pause, then Sadie strutted out in a royal-blue sequined evening gown. Her hair floated around her shoulders in soft waves, and she wore pale-blue eyeshadow and soft, pink lipstick.

"*Dios mío!*" Jenna exclaimed. "Sadie's stunning!" None of the girls could believe how glam she looked—a far cry from her usual sweats and her hair piled high in a ponytail.

Sadie tried her best not to wobble in the four-inch heels Mitchell had put her in, and when she got to the end of the runway, she winked at her PLC mates.

"Go, Sadie!" Kylie shouted. "Work it!"

Harold handed the camera to Marisol. "Go on. You take the photos of your friend in the finale."

"Me? I couldn't!" she insisted. "I mean, I'm not as good as you."

"And you won't be…unless you get more practice."

Marisol took Lucy and peered through the lens. She snapped shot after shot of Sadie strutting on the runway.

"Did you get it?" Harold asked her.

"I think so. It's hard to know for sure."

Harold shook his head. "You feel it in your bones," he replied. "When you get the shot, you know it."

Marisol took one last picture, just as Sadie pivoted on her heel and looked back over her shoulder at the audience, giving them a huge smile and wave.

"Got it!" Marisol said. "That's the one."

"Then that," Harold said, "is a wrap."

10

All Hands on Deck

The next morning, when the ship pulled into port in Florida, all the guests piled off the ship—all except for the cupcake club.

"The excursions are leaving," Delaney complained, peering out a porthole. She was wearing sunglasses with her baking apron. "I could be in Cinderella's castle by now."

"If we work straight through the day, we'll be ready for the pirate party tonight," Kylie assured her. "And then you can soak in the rays all day tomorrow in the Bahamas."

"Fine," Delaney sniffed. "But I'm not happy about missing the Magic Kingdom."

Once all the cupcakes were baked and decorated, all that was left was to build the raft.

"I know we did this once at Camp Chicopee," Kylie

said, scratching her head. "It was a team raft-building contest during Color War. Delaney, do you remember how we tied the logs together?"

"With rope…duh," Delaney snapped, still annoyed with having to miss a whole day of sun and fun.

Sadie, Kylie, and Jenna worked together, laying the logs on the floor and lacing rope between them while Lexi and Delaney put the finishing touches on the decorations for the remaining cupcakes.

"Are you sure it will float?" Jenna asked when they were done. "It looks a little flimsy." She tested it with her foot and a log rolled. "And slippery."

"It was strong enough to hold a pair of campers," Kylie insisted.

"Before it unraveled and we both fell in the lake," Delaney recalled.

Kylie had forgotten that part. "Well, we'll just make sure the knots are supertight and don't slip," she said.

They built a makeshift sail out of some wooden spoons and a baking apron, and Lexi drew a peace sign, heart, and cupcake on it to symbolize PLC.

"How many cupcakes do you think we can pile on?" Lexi asked.

Kylie held one in her hand. "There's only one way to find out."

They crammed more than five hundred cupcakes onto the raft. When Kylie checked the clock on the wall, it was nearly four p.m.—an hour before the ship was scheduled to pull out of port.

"We have just enough time to go get into our pirate outfits for the party," she said. "Phew! That was a close one."

Jenna wiped some dark chocolate from her hands on her apron. "Wait till you see the red silk blouse Mami made me. It'll go perfect with my eye patch, bandanna, and fake gold tooth."

"I don't care what I wear—as long as it's not another evening gown," Sadie vowed. "That gown last night weighed a ton! I'm wearing shorts for the rest of the cruise."

"Meet everyone on the Lido deck at seventeen hundred hours," Kylie said. "That's five p.m. in ship-speak."

"Aye, aye, Captain Kylie," Jenna teased. "I can't wait till our cupcakes set sail."

When the girls arrived on the pool deck, all the guests and crew were dressed for the costume party—with everything from peg legs and fake parrots on their shoulders to high buckle boots and tricornered black hats. There were evil pirates; silly pirates; swashbuckling pirates; pirates with beards and mustaches; pirates with feathered caps and knives in their teeth.

"This is crazy!" Lexi said. "People really got pirated up!" She had chosen to be a lady buccaneer in a red ruffled skirt, black boots, and a white blouse.

"Shiver me timbers, are those my fellow PLCers?" Delaney called, finding them in the crowd. She was dressed in a white puffy shirt and black jeans and wore a red ribbon tied across her forehead.

"Arrr!" Jenna growled back at her. Mami's red silk blouse was the perfect pirate attire, especially when she paired it with a black skirt and an eye patch. She grinned and flashed the girls her fake gold tooth. "Me name's Mad Medina," she said. "Queen of the High Seas."

"There's only one ruler of the high seas—and that's me," Kylie insisted. She had on a jacket with gold buttons and black boots and carried a sack of "pirate loot" slung over her back.

"What's in there?" Lexi teased her. "Gold doubloons?"

Kylie dug in the bag and pulled out a prop head,

dripping fake blood and guts. "Me latest victim—someone who dared to challenge Cap'n Kylie!"

"Eww!" Lexi ducked behind Sadie, whose costume paled in comparison. She was in a simple pair of black shorts and a white tank top, with a bandanna around her hair.

"That's awesome!" Delaney said enthusiastically. "How'd ya get the eyeballs to dangle like that?"

"Old horror-movie makeup trick," Kylie explained. "I'll show you sometime."

Mitchell pushed through all the guests to find them. "We're ready for you. The crew is carrying the cupcake raft to the pool, and Mr. Warren is super excited to see what you've done."

"Great!" Kylie said. "Cue the fog and the wind machine."

"And the spooky pirate music," Delaney reminded him.

"Anything else?" Mitchell seemed a tad annoyed to be taking orders yet again.

"Yeah," Kylie added. "Don't forget to announce us: 'the ghost ship *Peace, Love, and Cupcakes*, the terror of the seas!'"

Mitchell saluted her. "Whatever you say."

The girls readied themselves at the edge of the pool as the crew gently placed the raft on the top steps leading into it. The cupcakes had all survived the long walk up from the galley with not a bit of frosting out of place. "It's a miracle," Lexi said, relieved. "They look perfect." She glanced over and saw Mr. Warren—dressed as Captain Hook—giving them a thumbs-up.

Mitchell made the announcement over the loudspeaker. "Please turn your gaze to the giant Victory pool center deck for an amazing display…"

"Okay," Lexi instructed the girls. "On the count of three, we give it a gentle push into the pool."

"One…" Kylie said.

"Two…" Jenna continued.

"Three!" they all yelled in unison.

With a light push, the raft began to float from the steps into the shallow end of the pool.

"Steady…steady…" Sadie said, crossing her fingers.

It continued floating out into four feet, then six, then nine.

The crowd applauded enthusiastically. But that wasn't the end of the show. On Kylie's nod, the crew fired a confetti cannon that exploded over the onlookers in a burst of gold and silver.

"We did it!" Delaney exclaimed. "We actually did it."

Just then, a gust of wind rolled across the deck. Then another. Then another.

"Uh-oh," Kylie said, looking up. "Do those clouds look a little gray to you?"

"Never mind the weather report." Sadie pointed to the raft. "Our ship is about to tip!"

The wind had caused ripples in the pool, and the raft now rocked up and down uncontrollably.

"My cupcakes! My beautiful cupcakes!" Lexi moaned as a few toppled into the pool.

A few drops of rain landed on the deck.

"It's nothing," Mitchell assured the crowd. "Just a little sun shower."

With that, a bolt of lightning ripped across the sky and the winds began to kick up. Cupcakes were sliding off the raft and into the pool at an alarming rate.

"We have to do something," Kylie said, panicking. "We have to get the raft back to the shallow end and pull it out before all the cupcakes drown!"

"A captain always goes down with her ship," Jenna said, kicking off her black sandals. With that, she dove into the pool and tried to keep the raft steady.

"Swim it back to the steps!" Kylie called to her.

But the more Jenna tried to kick behind the raft and move it, the more the cupcakes tipped and toppled.

"What if you get under it?" Sadie shouted. "Like a turtle with a shell on its back?"

Jenna nodded and ducked beneath the raft. Slowly, the PLC pirate ship "swam" its way back to the shallow end where the girls could reach it.

"Whoa, you can hold your breath a really long time," Delaney acknowledged as Jenna finally popped up and out of the water. "Impressive!"

The guests didn't even seem to mind that the rain was now coming down harder and faster—they were mesmerized by Jenna's heroic show.

"All hail Mad Medina!" Delaney yelled.

Jenna climbed out of the pool, soaked to the bone. "It was nothing," she said.

"Oh, it was something!" Marisol interrupted her. "And I got lots of pictures to prove it."

Jenna's curls were all matted and stuck to her face. Her eye patch was hanging around her neck, and the beautiful blouse Mami had made her was a sopping wet. "Great," she said. "Next time, could you at least tell me to say cheese?"

Marisol held up her camera. "Say *queso*!" she teased her little sister.

Seas the Day

Once the party moved to the grand ballroom along with the remaining cupcakes, the girls were able to finally relax.

"I wouldn't call it a total disaster," Kylie said. She dug into a Jolly Roger raspberry and savored every bite. "At least most of the cupcakes stayed dry."

"Even if I didn't," Jenna said, bundling herself in a towel.

"I wouldn't call it a disaster at all." Mr. Warren suddenly appeared behind them. "Everyone is talking about that thrilling pirate show in the pool," he told them. "You made quite a splash, ladies."

Leo and Mitchell breathed a huge sigh of relief that their boss was pleased. "Pass me a cupcake," Mitchell told Kylie. "After all that drama, I need one." He popped three in his mouth, one after the other.

"Dark chocolate ganache," he said, licking his fingers. "My favorite."

"So what are your plans for the rest of the cruise—now that you're off duty?" Leo asked the club.

"Sun and fun," Delaney said. "Finally!"

"About that…" Mitchell interrupted her. "The forecast is calling for rain tomorrow."

Delaney rolled her eyes. "I give up. I just give up."

"We'll still have plenty of time in the Bahamas, and the captain promised me he'd make a special stop in Florida on the way home since some of our VIPs missed their excursion to Disney World."

"Yes!" Delaney pumped her fist in the air. "Magic Kingdom, here I come!"

Jenna made a face. "Do you think we could maybe skip the Pirates of the Caribbean ride?" she asked her friends. "I think I've had enough adventure on the high seas for one trip."

Meanwhile, Harold had a chance to flip through the images Marisol had taken with his camera.

"These are excellent," he told her. "You truly have an eye."

Marisol shrugged. "Ya think?"

"I do," he replied. "And I have a surprise for you. Be at the lobby tomorrow morning and you'll see."

Marisol had no idea what Harold was planning—but she realized she couldn't lie to him anymore.

"Mr. Hammond," she began. "About Lucy…"

"You got her wet," he said. "I saw some condensation inside the lens while I was shooting."

"I'm so sorry. It was stupid and irresponsible, and I wouldn't blame you for never trusting me with your equipment again."

"Well, that would be a problem," he replied. "You see, I've decided to come out of retirement, and I'll be needing an assistant to help me this summer. I was hoping you'd be interested—and I'll pay you for whatever shoots you come along on."

Marisol's face lit up. "You mean it? That would be amazing!"

"Of course," he reminded her, "you'll need to get your parents' permission."

Marisol sighed. "That means telling my mom that I'm not going to be a doctor."

"I think she'd rather hear the truth from you than lies," Harold said. "I know I would. And after tomorrow, I think you'll have an easier way to tell her."

Immediately after breakfast, Marisol, Maggie, Jenna, and the rest of PLC filed into the ship's lobby. There were chairs set around a stage.

"What do you suppose that is?" Jenna asked her sister. She pointed to what looked like several easels draped in cloths.

"I don't know. Harold said it was a surprise."

Kylie checked the ship's daily schedule. "It says 9:00 a.m. art exhibit."

Guests began filling up the chairs in anticipation. Leo and Harold walked up on the stage to introduce the event.

"It gives me great pleasure to introduce one of the finest photographers in the world, Mr. Harold Hammond," Leo said in the microphone.

Harold bowed modestly. "This exhibit is not about me," he told the audience. "It's about a young talent that I've discovered right here on this ship." He pulled a cloth off one of the easels to reveal one of the shots Marisol had taken of Sadie in the fashion show. Then he yanked off another: this time, it was a photo of Jenna midair diving into the pool to save her cupcakes.

86

The crowd oohed and aahed. Each photo he unveiled was Marisol's.

"Marisol Medina"—he pointed at her—"please come up here and take a bow."

"Go! Go!" Jenna said, giving her a push.

Leo looked utterly stunned. "Marisol," he said, admiring the prints. "These are amazing. Your mother is going to be so proud of you."

"Really?" Marisol asked. "You don't think she'll be mad that I don't want to be a doctor?"

Leo gasped. "You mean…you don't want to go to pre-med in college?"

Marisol took a deep breath. "No, not really. I thought I did for the longest time, but it's not where my heart is. And someone told me I should follow *mis sueños*." She looked at Jenna.

"Well, that's big news," Leo said.

"Do you think Mami will understand?" Marisol asked him.

He took her hand. "I think she'll be bursting with pride that her daughter is going to be a famous photographer one day."

Marisol smiled. It felt so good not to have to lie anymore.

"Thank you," she said, hugging Harold. "I don't know what to say."

"Say you'll do me proud," he told her. "And I owe you a lot too. You reminded me of how sad I've been since I put my dreams away on the shelf."

When the ship finally docked back in New York, Betty, Gabby, and the twins were waiting to greet the rest of their family. The pier was in a state of happy chaos: besides the people waiting and long lines of taxis, there were huge crowds of guests piling off the ship with luggage and souvenirs.

Leo scanned the crowd, searching for his wife.

"*Aquí!* Over here!" Betty shouted.

"I missed you, *mi amor*," Leo said, swooping sweeping Betty into his arms and kissing her. "All of you." He handed each of the twins a plastic pirate sword, and they instantly began fighting with them.

"Look," Gabby said, hugging Jenna. "All my polka dots are almost gone."

"Mine too!" Ricky said, taking a break from his duel.

"No more chicken pops!" Manny added.

Marisol hung back, waiting to greet her mom.

"*Mija!*" Betty held her arms out to her. "How was your trip?"

"Great," Marisol said. "And I have something for you."

She handed Betty a framed photo she had taken of a sunset across the ocean. The vibrant colors practically jumped out of the picture.

"This is beautiful," her mother said. "You bought this for me?"

"I took that photo, Mami," Marisol said slowly.

"You? You took this?" Betty held in her hands and stared. "*Eres muy talentoso!*"

"She *is* very talented," Jenna piped up. "And she's gonna be a famous photographer one day."

"A photographer?" Mami asked, confused.

Marisol gulped. "*Sí*, Mami. If it's okay with you. I want to go to college and study photojournalism."

Betty said nothing; she just stared. "A famous photo-journalist? In our family? *Que maravilloso!*"

"You mean you're not disappointed I won't be a doc-tor?" Marisol asked.

"*Mija*, we're proud of you no matter what you do," Leo assured her. "And it takes a lot of courage to follow your dreams."

"*Sí*," Betty added. "As long as you're happy, I'm happy."

Jenna gave Marisol a little nudge. "Told ya so."

"Marisol, wait!" Harold caught up to her just as they were leaving the terminal. "You forgot something." He handed her Lucy.

"Your camera? I can't! I almost destroyed it!"

"Which means you'll be much more careful with her now—especially since I'm giving her to you to keep."

"Take it." Jenna nudged Marisol again.

Kylie nodded. "Marisol, we could really use someone to shoot pictures for our new PLC website."

Marisol beamed and pointed her camera at the cupcake club for one last shot from the cruise. "Say 'cupcake!'" she said with a *click*!

George Washington's Cherry Cupcakes

The first prez would have flipped over these flavorful cupcakes!

Cherry Cupcakes

Makes 24 cupcakes

   1½ cups sugar

   ½ cup (1 stick) unsalted butter (I prefer Plugrá),
      room temperature

   4 egg whites, room temperature

   1½ teaspoons vanilla extract

   2 cups cake flour

   1½ teaspoons baking powder

   ½ teaspoon baking soda

   ½ teaspoon salt

   1⅓ cups buttermilk

   10 ounces (1 jar) maraschino cherries,
      finely chopped

2 tablespoons maraschino cherry juice (leftover
   from the jar)

Directions

1. Preheat oven to 350°F. Line two muffin pans with
    cupcake liners.

2. In the large bowl of an electric mixer set on high
    speed, cream together the sugar and butter until
    light and fluffy.

3. Reduce to low speed, and slowly add the egg
    whites one at a time. Add the vanilla, and mix
    until combined.

4. In a separate bowl, whisk together the flour, baking
    powder, baking soda, and salt.

5. Slowly add the dry ingredients to the butter mix-
    ture, beating at low speed for approximately two
    minutes until the batter is smooth.

6. In another small bowl, stir together the buttermilk
    and cherry juice. With the mixer on low, slowly add
    this mixture to the batter in the large bowl.

7. Add the chopped cherries, mixing slowly until they
    are blended into the batter.

8. Fill the cupcake liners about three-quarters full

with the batter. Bake for 18–20 minutes, or until a toothpick inserted into the center of a cupcake comes out clean.

9. Allow the cupcakes to cool completely, about 15 minutes, before frosting.

Pink Perfection Frosting

Here's how to make a cotton candy–colored shade of icing to top off your cherry cupcake.

3½ cups confectioners' sugar

1 cup unsalted butter, room temperature

⅛ teaspoon salt

1 teaspoon milk

1 teaspoon vanilla extract

4 to 6 drops red food coloring

Directions

1. In a bowl combine sugar, butter, and salt. Beat until blended.

2. Add the milk and vanilla, and beat for an additional three to five minutes, or until smooth and creamy.

3. Add 4 to 6 drops of red food coloring. (Six will give

you more of a bubble gum color, while 4 will be more pastel.) Mix until fully blended, then frost your cupcakes. Can you say "Yum"?

PLC's Wonderful White Chocolate Cupcakes

A rich yet delicate chocolate cupcake that feels fancy!

White Chocolate Cupcakes

Makes 24 cupcakes

  6 ounces white chocolate, finely chopped

  ⅔ cup sugar

  4 tablespoons butter (½ stick), room temperature

  2 eggs

  1½ cups all-purpose flour

  1 teaspoon baking powder

  ½ teaspoon salt

  1 cup milk

  1 tablespoon vanilla extract

Directions

  1. Preheat oven to 350°F. Line two muffin pans with cupcake liners.

2. Ask a parent to help you melt the white chocolate, either in a double boiler or (the easy way!) in a microwave oven. Set your microwave at 50 percent power so you don't scorch the chocolate. Place the chocolate in a microwave-safe bowl. Heat for 30 seconds, then remove and stir. Careful! The bowl will be hot. Continue heating in 30-second intervals, stirring as needed, until the melted chocolate is smooth and creamy.

3. In the large bowl of a mixer, cream the sugar and butter together on low speed to combine, then on high until the mixture becomes light and fluffy.

4. Reduce the speed to low, and slowly add the eggs one at a time.

5. Beat in the melted chocolate.

6. In another bowl, whisk together the flour, baking powder, and salt until combined.

7. In a small bowl, stir together the milk and vanilla.

8. With the mixer on low speed, add the flour mixture and the milk mixture, alternating between them until the batter is smooth and creamy. You may need to scrape down the sides of the bowl with a spatula to make sure everything is combined.

9. Fill the cupcake liners about three-quarters full with the batter. Bake for 18–20 minutes, or until a toothpick inserted into the center of a cupcake comes out clean.

10. Allow the cupcakes to cool completely, about 15 minutes, before frosting.

Chocolate Ganache

9 ounces semisweet chocolate, coarsely chopped

1 cup heavy cream

Directions

1. Ask an adult to help you, since this requires heating the chocolate and cream on a stove top. Place the chocolate into a medium bowl.

2. Heat the cream in a small saucepan over medium heat. Bring just to a boil. Watch carefully; it will boil fast!

3. When the cream has come to a boil, pour it over the chopped chocolate, and whisk until smooth.

4. Let the ganache cool slightly, then pour it into a large bowl.

5. Dip each cupcake top into the ganache. Make sure

the chocolate coats the entire top. (It may take more than one dip.) You can then add sprinkles, colored sugar, or any other decorations your heart desires! Personally, I love ripe, fresh raspberries!

Pirate Pistachio Cupcakes

Your friends will be "green with envy" when you whip up this recipe!

Pistachio Cupcakes
Makes 12 cupcakes

- 1½ cups all-purpose flour
- 1 box instant pistachio pudding (I used Jell-O)
- 1½ teaspoons baking powder
- ½ teaspoon salt
- ⅔ cup sugar
- ½ cup (1 stick) unsalted butter, room temperature
- 1 teaspoon vanilla extract
- 1 teaspoon vegetable oil
- 2 eggs
- 1 egg white
- ½ cup milk

Directions

1. Preheat oven to 350°F. Line a muffin pan with cupcake liners and set aside.

2. In a mixing bowl, whisk or mix flour, baking powder, salt, and instant pudding together until well combined.

3. In the large bowl of an electric mixer set on high speed, cream the sugar and butter together until light and fluffy. Add the vanilla and vegetable oil.

4. With the mixer on low, add in the eggs and egg white, one at a time.

5. Add in the flour mixture and milk, alternating between them. Scrape the sides of the bowl with a spatula to make sure all ingredients are combined. The batter should be smooth and creamy.

6. Fill the cupcake liners three-quarters full with batter. Bake for 18–20 minutes or until a toothpick inserted into the center of a cupcake comes out clean.

7. Allow the cupcakes to cool completely, about 15 minutes, before frosting. I like to use a basic vanilla buttercream (see the recipe for pink perfection frosting on page pages 95 and 96) and add a few drops of green food coloring to give it that real pistachio

feel. If you're going for a pirate theme, why not add a skull-and-crossbones flag that you color, cut out, and tape to a toothpick? Just insert it in the frosted cupcake, and yo-ho-ho, you're ready to go!

Carrie's Q & A: Vinny Buzzetta, Cake Artist Extraordinaire!

Vinny Buzzetta was one of the very first cake masters I interviewed for my *Carrie's Cupcake Critique* blog. Vinny also baked cupcakes for one of my Halloween parties and created oozing eyeballs and blood on them. *So cool!* What's even more impressive is that he has been baking professionally since he was a teenager and was boss of his own biz before he was even twenty-one. After graduating from high school, he attended the French Culinary Institute of NYC and graduated from the classic pastry arts program.

Following that, he opened up The Cake Artist, a custom cake and cupcake shop on Staten Island, and filmed a reality series, *Staten Island Cakes*. He's now a freelance cake artist and has done many different pastry projects, including work with Daffy's, Bergdorf Goodman, Ralph Lauren, the New York City Ballet, and more. He promises me that he's looking for a space to open a new bakery in NYC. (Hurry up! Please!)

Carrie: Vinny, what makes the perfect cupcake?

Vinny: In my opinion, the perfect cupcake first and foremost has to be delicious and moist. Of course, an aesthetically pleasing cupcake is great, but if it's dry and tasteless, then what's the point? The perfect cupcake should be sweet and buttery and light as a feather, topped with delicious, flavorful cream. Any artistic decorations are just a plus!

Carrie: You're known for your amazing cake decorating, and your cupcakes are works of art as well. What's the coolest cupcake topper you've ever done?

Vinny: Recently, a friend of mine launched a new baby product called Baby Soothe, an infant massaging device, and she hired me to re-create it in sugar on top of cupcakes for her launch party. Over the years I've done many different cupcake toppers, but this one I certainly enjoyed. I think her product looked better in sugar than in real life! I was thrilled to help a good friend out.

Carrie: What are your fave flavors of cupcakes? What are the most popular ones you sell?

Vinny: In all honesty, I love them all! I have the biggest sweet tooth and couldn't turn down any flavor. If I had to pick just one, it would have to be something chocolate. Chocolate *anything*! I'll admit I am a total chocoholic! As far as the most popular, my Oreo cupcakes are killer. They're the number one cake and cupcake flavor requested.

Carrie: How did you first start baking and decorating cakes? Who taught you?

Vinny: I've always had a passion for baking and desserts, ever since I can remember. My first mentor was Carol Frazzetta of Carol's Cafe on Staten Island. I started taking classes at her restaurant when I was just fourteen! From there she hired me to be a pastry sous chef in her kitchen. I would assist her in baking desserts for the restaurant. I really developed a solid foundation for desserts with her. She taught me so much and really inspired me to become who I am today. As far as cakes go, I am really a self-taught designer. Although I attended culinary school, I just learned the basics there. I remember always watching *Food Network Challenge* from a young age and learning by trial and error from that. Somehow it worked!

Carrie: You started out really young as a pastry chef with your own biz. What advice do you have for kids who want to grow up to own their own bakeries?

Vinny: My advice to all young kids aspiring to be a pastry chef is *do it*! Don't let any obstacles come in your way and stop you. I've had many trials and tribulations over the years, and I never let anything get in the way of my passion. From fighting my parents to go to culinary school to opening up my first business. I persevered and pushed until I reached my goals! I love what I do and wouldn't want my life any other way! Chase your dreams and turn them into a reality.

Acknowledgments

Many thanks to all our family and friends who make "Cupcake" possible:

The Kahns, Berks, and Saperstones, as always, for their love and support. Daddy and Maddie: love you to the moon and back!

Our supersweet agents, Katherine Latshaw and Frank Weimann from Folio Lit; our great team at Sourcebooks Jabberwocky: Steve Geck, Kate Prosswimmer, Alex Yeadon, Elizabeth Boyer.

All of our Cupcake Club fans who come to every signing, preorder, and race to bookstores the day the next book is out, and share their enthusiasm for the series with us! Hugs and sprinkles!

About the Authors

Sheryl Berk is the *New York Times* bestselling coauthor of *Soul Surfer*. An entertainment editor and journalist, she has written dozens of books with celebrities, including Britney Spears, Jenna Ushkowitz, and Zendaya. Her daughter, Carrie Berk, is a renowned cupcake connoisseur and blogger (www.facebook.com/PLCCupcakeClub; www.carriescupcakecritique.shutterfly.com; Instagram @plccupcakeclub) with over 105K followers at the tender young age of twelve! Carrie cooked up the idea for the Cupcake Club series while in second grade. To date, she and Sheryl have written eleven books together (with many more in the works!). *Peace, Love, and Cupcakes* had its world premiere as a delicious new musical at New York City's Vital Theatre in 2014. The Berk ladies are also hard at work on a new series, Fashion Academy, as well as its musical version—*Fashion Academy: The Musical*, premiering October 2015 in NYC.

Peace Love and Cupcakes

Meet Kylie Carson.

She's a fourth grader with a big problem. How will she make friends at her new school? Should she tell her classmates she loves monster movies? Forget it. Play the part of a turnip in the school play? Disaster! Then Kylie comes up with a delicious idea: What if she starts a cupcake club?

Soon Kylie's club is spinning out tasty treats with the help of her fellow bakers and new friends. But when Meredith tries to sabotage the girls' big cupcake party, will it be the end of the cupcake club?

Book
1

Recipe For Trouble

$\mathcal{M}$eet Lexi Poole.

To Lexi, a new school year means back to baking with her BFFs in the cupcake club. But the club president, Kylie, is mixing things up by inviting new members. And Lexi is in for a not-so-sweet surprise when she is cast in the school's production of *Romeo and Juliet*. If only she could be as confident onstage as she is in the kitchen. The icing on the cake: her secret crush is playing Romeo. Sounds like a recipe for trouble!

Can the girls' friendship stand the heat, or will the cupcake club go up in smoke?

Book
2

Winner Bakes All

$\mathcal{M}$eet Sadie.

When she's not mixing it up on the basketball court, she's mixing the perfect batter with her friends in the cupcake club. Sadie's definitely no stranger to competition, but the oven mitts are off when the club is chosen to appear on *Battle of the Bakers*, the ultimate cupcake competition on TV. If the girls want a taste of sweet victory, they'll have to beat the very best bakers. But the real battle happens off camera when the club's baking business starts losing money. Long recipe short, no money for icing and sprinkles means no cupcake club.

With the clock ticking and the cameras rolling, will the club and their cupcakes rise to the occasion?

Book
3

Icing on the Cake

Meet Jenna.

She's the cupcake club's official taste tester, but the past few weeks have not been so sweet. Her mom just got engaged to Leo—who Jenna is sure is not "The One"—and Peace, Love, and Cupcakes has to bake the wedding cake. Jenna is ready to throw in the towel, especially when she hears the wedding will be in Las Vegas on Easter weekend, one of the most important holidays for the club's business!

Can Jenna and her friends handle their busy orders—and the Elvis impersonators—or will they have a cupcake meltdown?

Book
4

Baby Cakes

$\mathcal{M}$eet Delaney.

New cupcake club member Delaney is shocked to find out her mom is expecting twins! When her parents first tell her, the practical joker thinks they must be pulling her leg. For ten years she's had her parents—and her room—all to herself. She LIKED being an only child. But now she's going to be a big sis.

The girls of Peace, Love, and Cupcakes get together to bake cupcakes and discover Delaney is worried about what kind of a big sister she will be. She's never even babysat before! But her cupcake club friends rally to her side for a crash course in Big Sister 101.

Book
5

Royal Icing

Meet Kylie.

As the founder and president of Peace, Love, and Cupcakes, Kylie's kept the club going through all kinds of sticky situations. But when PLC's advisor surprises the group with an impromptu trip to London, the rest of the group jumps on board—without even asking Kylie. All of sudden, Kylie's noticing the club doesn't need their president nearly as much as they used to. To top it off, the girls get an order for two thousand cupcakes from Lady Wakefield of Wilshire herself—to be presented in the shape of the London Bridge! Talk about a royal challenge...

Can Kylie figure out her place in the club in time to prevent their London Bridge—and PLC—from falling down?

Book 6

Sugar and Spice

$\mathcal{M}$eet Lexi.

The girls of Peace, Love, and Cupcakes might be sugar and spice and everything nice, but the same can't be said for Meredith, whose favorite hobby is picking on Lexi. So when the PLC gets a cupcake order from the New England Shooting Starz—the beauty pageant Meredith is competing in—the girls have a genius idea: enter Lexi into the competition so she can show Meredith once and for all that she's no better than anyone else. Problem is, PLC has to make Lexi a pageant queen—and 1,000 cupcakes—all in a matter of weeks!

Have the girls of Peace, Love, and Cupcakes bitten off more than they can chew?

Book
7

Sweet Victory

Meet Sadie.

MVP Sadie knows what it takes to win—both on the court and in the kitchen. But when Coach Walsh gets sick and has to temporarily leave school, Sadie's suddenly at a loss. What will she do without Coach's spot-on advice and uplifting encouragement? Luckily, Sadie's got Peace, Love, and Cupcakes on her side. Her friends know that the power of friendship—and cupcakes—might be just what Sadie needs! Together, they rally to whip up the largest batch of sweet treats they've ever made, all to help support Coach Walsh. When the going gets tough, a little PLC goes a long way. But this record-breaking order might just be too much for the club...

Can the girls pull it together in time to score a win for Sadie—and Coach Walsh?

Book
8